PRINCESS CANDY

SUGAR HERO

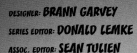

DESIGNER: **BRANN GARVEY**

SERIES EDITOR: **DONALD LEMKE**

ASSOC. EDITOR: **SEAN TULIEN**

ART DIRECTOR: **BOB LENTZ**

CREATIVE DIRECTOR: **HEATHER KINDSETH**

PRODUCTION SPECIALIST: **MICHELLE BIEDSCHEID**

Raintree is an imprint of Capstone Global Library Limited, a company incorporated in England and Wales having its registered office at 264 Banbury Road, Oxford, OX2 7DY – Registered company number: 6695582

www.raintree.co.uk
myorders@raintree.co.uk

Text © Capstone Global Library Limited 2019
The moral rights of the proprietor have been asserted

ISBN 978 1 4747 8230 2
22 21 20 19
10 9 8 7 6 5 4 3 2 1

Printed and bound in India

British Library Cataloguing in Publication Data
A full catalogue record for this book is available from the British Library.

PRINCESS CANDY

SUGAR HERO

WRITTEN BY
MICHAEL DAHL

ILLUSTRATED BY
JEFF CROWTHER

DOOZIE HISS

MR. SLINK

Midnight is a place.

A big, dark city.

And in one corner of Midnight City, in Midnight School . . .

Something weird is going on.

Something so scary . . .

Something so hairy . . .

That we can't even look!

Dear Halo,
You are my favourite niece. That is why I am giving you this special, secret gift. It was given to me long ago, on my eleventh birthday.

As you know, I am very ill. In case anything should happen to me, I have left this gift with Grandma. She will give it to you on YOUR eleventh birthday. Remember to use it wisely.

"Your loving aunt, Pandora."

Use it wisely? What does that mean?

Back at their flat, Halo gets ready for bed . . .

Sweets? I don't get it. Aunt Pandora always told me to eat fruits and vegetables.

And I wonder what's so special about it?

Well, it certainly looks pretty.

And I think *fuego* means "fire".

I'll just try one.

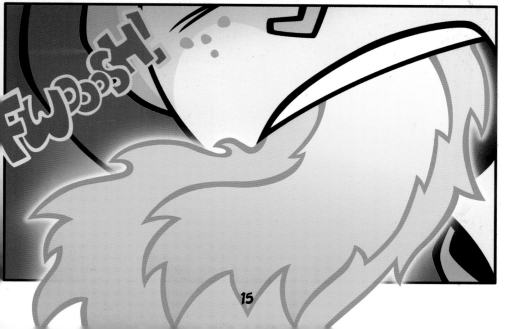

Hi, Grandma. I've almost finished my homework. I'll be outside in a few minutes.

Good girl. I'll be parked by the front door.

I didn't find out anything about Aunt Pandora's sweets in the school's science books.

Maybe I'll go to the town library tomorr —

MR. SLINK

Hey, what's that!?

23

25

26

27

28

Thanks again for the lift, Grandma.

No problem, Halo.

Hey, I have an idea.

How about us girls go to the beauty salon tomorrow?

We could both get our hair done.

Hair?

About The Author

Michael Dahl is the author of more than 200 books for children and young adults. He has won the AEP Distinguished Achievement Award three times for his non-fiction. His Finnegan Zwake mystery series was shortlisted twice by the Anthony and Agatha awards. He has also written the Library of Doom series and the Dragonblood books. He speaks at US conferences about graphic novels and high-interest books for boys.

About The Illustrator

Jeff Crowther has been drawing comics for as long as he can remember. Since graduating from college, Jeff has worked on a variety of illustrations for clients including Disney, Adventures Magazine and Boy's Life Magazine. He also wrote and illustrated the webcomic Sketchbook and has self-published several mini-comics. Jeff lives in Ohio, USA, with his wife, Elizabeth, and their children, Jonas and Noelle.

Glossary

aqua a Spanish word meaning "water"

average usual, or ordinary

charcoal a form of carbon made from partially burned wood, often used as barbecue fuel

fuego a Spanish word meaning "fire"

powerful having great strength

pressure a burden or strain

property anything that is owned by an individual

wisely to do something with good judgment

woozy feeling dizzy or mildly sick

Doozie Hiss

SUPER-VILLAIN

Villain facts

First appearance
Princess Candy: Sugar Hero

Real name...............Medusa Marie Hiss

Occupation............................Top student

Height......................................1.3 metres

Weight................................34 kilograms

Eyes..Black

Hair......................Green (and snake-like)

Special powers
Super-annoying personality; ability to
instantly transform into a teacher's pet;
living hair with deadly tentacle powers

Unable to have another child, Medusa's parents
spoiled their only daughter rotten. On the
morning of her year three class photo, Medusa
woke up to a particularly bad hair day. Her mother,
a genetic scientist, created a high-tech hair gel to
tame her child's unruly hairdo. But after her father,
an out-of-work hairdresser, applied the prototype
product, Medusa's hair turned deadly. With her
lizard locks, she had become the evil and annoying
. . . Doozie Hiss.

PRINCESS PUZZLERS

Q: Where does the word "candy" come from?

A: The word "candy" comes from the Arabic word "qandi", which means "sugar".

Q: Who discovered chocolate?

A: People from the ancient cultures of Mexico and Central America made chocolate more than 2,000 years ago.

Q: How big was the largest lollipop ever made?

A: The largest lollipop ever was made in California, USA, in 2012. It weighed 3176.5 kilograms!

Discussion Questions

1. Halo caught Doozie Hiss stealing the answers to a test. What do you think Doozie's punishment should be? Explain your answer.

2. Why do you think Aunt Pandora chose to give Halo the super-powered sweets? What do you think she wanted Halo to do with them?

3. When she eats a sweet, Halo gains some amazing superpowers. If you could have just one superpower, what would it be? Explain.

WRITING PROMPTS

1. Think about your favourite sweets. Now imagine that sweet treat could turn you into a superhero. Write about what you would do with your new-found powers.

2. At the end of the story, Halo leaves Doozie tied to the flagpole. Pretend you are the author and write a story about what happens next. Does Doozie escape? Is she punished for her crime?

3. Write your own Princess Candy comic. What kind of sweets will Halo try next time? What super-villlain will she face? Use your imagination.